# Praise for *The Gratitude Express*

**"Walter Green has lived a life worth living. I love the way he sees the world and how he lives his life. Of all the biohacking and longevity obsession going on these days, few if any are talking about having meaningful relationships and expressing our gratitude for their impact on our lives. Let us be grateful for Walter and *The Gratitude Express*!"**

—**SIMON SINEK,** #1 *NEW YORK TIMES* AND *WALL STREET JOURNAL* BESTSELLING AUTHOR AND TED SPEAKER

**"*The Gratitude Express* is a powerful and poignant tale that vividly demonstrates the transformative power of gratitude—an essential (but increasingly forgotten) glue that binds us humans together as a bonded social species. Simply put, it urges us all to 'say it now' and enrich our lives and the lives of others with heartfelt appreciation."**

—**MATTHEW WALKER, PhD,** PROFESSOR AT UNIVERSITY OF CALIFORNIA, BERKELEY

**"*The Gratitude Express*, written by my good friend Walter Green, is a little book with a big lesson: Life is short and unpredictable. If you have something you want to say to a friend or loved one, you should say it now! My wife, Margie, and I agree. We tell people, 'Keep your I love yous up to date.' Nobody knows what the future holds. Thanks, Walter, for the loving wake-up call we all need."**

—**KEN BLANCHARD, PhD,** BESTSELLING AUTHOR

**"Walter Green takes a simple concept and transforms it into some of the most powerful moments we as humans can experience. *The Gratitude Express* reminds us that we often wait too late to tell the people in our lives the tremendous impact they've had on us. This book reinvents the way we embrace gratitude and shift humanity in a time when we need it most. This actionable, inspiring book helps foster deeper connections with the individuals that have helped shape our lives."**

—**CYNTHIA THURLOW,** NURSE PRACTITIONER AND BESTSELLING AUTHOR

**"*The Gratitude Express* by Walter Green is a touching journey about the power of gratitude. In a world where most of us live somewhere between guilt from our past and anxiety about our future, this story demonstrates the importance of living in the present and using love as our main language. The inspiring message lingers long after the final page, prompting us to reflect on the significance of fostering connections and embracing moments of gratitude in our own lives."**

—**RIC ELIAS,** CEO OF RED VENTURES AND "MIRACLE ON THE HUDSON" SURVIVOR

**"'Say It Now' is a beautiful invitation to slow down, reflect on the extraordinary people who have enriched our lives, and share our gratitude in meaningful ways. It's a powerful catalyst for strengthening bonds, mending relationships, and living with greater fulfillment by acknowledging the generosity and goodness around us."**

—**CRAIG KIELBURGER,** *NEW YORK TIMES* BESTSELLING AUTHOR AND GLOBAL SOCIAL ENTREPRENEUR

“Walter Green’s message in *The Gratitude Express* has revolutionized the way we view gratitude across the globe. Why we wait until someone passes to tell them how they’ve enhanced our lives is an antiquated tradition that only leads to a life of regret. ‘Say It Now’ is the answer humanity needs today to conquer our most challenging times. It changed my life and how I live.”

—**CHAITRA VEDULLAPALLI,** CMO, MEYLAH, *FORBES* 1000 NEXT ENTREPRENEUR, AND GLOBAL SPEAKER

“What a gift Walter Green gives us with this fabulous book! He illustrates that we should always give without remembering and receive without forgetting. This is an inspiring reminder to us all on how to learn, live, and be grateful.”

—**NIDO R. QUBEIN,** PRESIDENT, HIGH POINT UNIVERSITY

# *The Gratitude Express*

A Story Inspired by the **Say It Now Movement**

*WALTER GREEN*

*with* JOSEPH QUADERER *illustrations by* WADE FORBES

say it
now

*The Gratitude Express*



Second printing. This edition printed in 2026.

This is a work of fiction. Names, characters, businesses, places, events, and incidents are either the products of the author's imagination or used in a fictitious manner. Any resemblance to actual persons, living or dead, or actual events is purely coincidental.

**For more information, please contact:**
Amplify Publishing Group
620 Herndon Parkway, Suite 220
Herndon, VA 20170
info@amplifypublishing.com

Library of Congress Control Number: 2025916058

CPSIA Code: PRV0226B

ISBN-13: 979-8-89138-525-2

Printed in the United States

To my beloved wife, Lola, who has either created or enthusiastically supported everything that has been important in my business and personal life.

Say It Now evolved over thirty-five years, and each step of the way Lola left her imprint. Words can neither do her justice nor adequately express the full measure of my love and gratitude.

Our greatest achievement and our most important legacy have been our twin sons, Jon and Jason. Jason and our daughter-in-law, Ann, have bestowed upon us our grandchildren, Claire and Wilson, the priceless gift of joy in the present and hope for the future.

—WALTER GREEN

"Expressing gratitude to someone is one of life's greatest treasures. It's a universal language that has the power to transform and deepen our relationships with one another and discover the impact we have had on the lives we've touched. There is no greater gift we can give to others and to ourselves. This is the legacy we are creating today that will pass on to generations when we are no longer here. The story you are about to experience illuminates the power of saying it now."

—MARTIN LUTHER KING III

# I

Beacon was a town nestled in a wide valley, with a strong blue river running through it and mountains arching high into the sky.

Daniel stood on the platform at Beacon train station. He was taking the train to visit his grandfather, who lived four stops away. He'd made the trip many times before, but this time was different.

In his hand he held a notebook in a thick

leather binder. It was filled with thoughts, reflections, and ideas.

Although Daniel was a journalist, he'd sat down at his desk from noon until midnight the previous day, struggling with what to write. It wasn't that he had too little to say; it was that he had *too much*. He was writing a eulogy to be used after his grandpa passed, and he struggled to condense a lifetime of influence into a few pages.

He flipped the notebook open to the first page and read the only line he knew he'd keep for sure: *Grandpa, you have no idea the difference you've made in my life . . .*

A picture fell out and landed on the terminal floor. Daniel picked it up and looked at it.

He was just a little boy in the photo. He and his grandfather had walked through a field after the year's first snowfall—white, glistening snow covered everything like a frosted candy shell. They built a snowman together and then took a picture. Daniel stood on one side of the snowman; his grandfather stood on the other, wearing a wise, knowing smirk.

Daniel rubbed the old photo between his fingers, then he wedged it into the leather-bound notebook and hugged it tight to his chest. *Grandpa, you have no idea the difference you've made in my life*, he repeated to himself.

Suddenly, Daniel was shaken from his reverie by a strange noise—a puffing and hissing that reverberated off the mountains and echoed through the valley. Just when he thought he'd imagined the sounds, he heard the short, shrill blast of a steam locomotive whistle. Daniel glanced in the direction of the noise and saw a billowing plume of steam rising high into the sky.

Moments later an antique train hissed and chugged into the station—all polished brass and gleaming metal. Daniel smelled the scent of steam, coal, and oil. When the locomotive passed in front of him, he felt the vibrations deep in his chest, and the heat from the engine warmed his face.

Daniel glanced around to see if anyone else was there to witness this oddity, but he was curiously the only person at the station. *Had he ever before been alone at this station?* he wondered. He didn't think so.

Daniel looked at his watch—5:07. He glanced at the train bulletin board, and it was the usual 5:15 to Cedarville—where his grandfather lived—but no mention of a 5:07 train. And certainly, there was no mention of an antique steam train. Again, Daniel glanced around, but there was nobody else to ask.

The train creaked to a stop, and a conductor stepped down the stairs and onto the station platform. He wore a bold blue uniform with a vest and a peaked conductor's hat. His face had a wise yet welcoming warmth about it. But, most surprisingly, the conductor had a bird on his shoulder—a bright red parrot with white cheeks and a beautiful blue chest.

"Where to, young man?"

Daniel was startled.

The conductor took a pocket watch out of his vest and glanced at it. He moved with an oiled efficiency.

"Now, now, young man." He raised his eyes to Daniel. "We have a schedule to keep. Where to?"

"Yeah," the parrot squawked, "where to?"

When the parrot spoke, the plumes on its head spiked.

"Cedarville," Daniel stammered. "Is this train going to Cedarville? The 5:15 local to Cedarville?"

"This is the 5:07 Gratitude Express," the conductor said and pointed at the brass emblem on his hat.

Daniel squinted and could finally make out the words: Gratitude Express.

"Does it stop at Cedarville?"

"Making all stops!" the conductor bellowed and glanced at his pocket watch again. "All aboard!"

"All aboard!" the parrot squawked as the conductor turned around and climbed onto the mysterious train.

"Making all stops?" Daniel mumbled to himself as he stepped onto the train.

No sooner had he boarded than the train jolted forward and the steam whistle let out a blast that echoed off the mountains.

# II

The inside of the train was empty, and it smelled like old leather, oil, and smoke. The interior was curious—large, rectangular windows of heavy glass lined both sides of the passenger car. Rather than facing forward, the rows of seats were pressed against the sides of the train. A large wooden table—polished to a shine—was bolted in the center of the floor. Daniel put his notebook on the table and sat down on one of the leather seats.

Shortly after, the conductor, with the parrot on his shoulder, walked through the door.

Daniel had been so preoccupied with thoughts about his grandfather that he forgot to buy a ticket.

He told the train conductor that he didn't have a ticket.

The conductor said, "You can't buy a ticket for this train because none are required."

The conductor pulled a thick wad of paper out of his rear pocket.

"Cedarville?" he asked without looking up.

Daniel said yes.

The conductor punched one ticket in the center and handed it to Daniel.

The ticket punch said, "Express Gratitude."

Suddenly the train lurched, and Daniel's notebook was thrown onto the floor—notes, pictures, and scraps scattered everywhere.

Daniel was on his hands and knees collecting everything when he heard the parrot speak.

"What's that?" the parrot asked.

"It's a notebook."

"I know," squawked the parrot, "but what's *inside?*"

Daniel looked up, and both the conductor and the parrot were staring at him expectantly.

"Sorry, he's a very curious bird."

"I'm writing a eulogy," Daniel said, "for my grandfather. He's ill."

"What's a eulogy?" the parrot squawked.

"It's a speech where you share your appreciation for someone who has made a difference in your life after they have passed away."

"Why wait until someone dies to say nice things about them?" the parrot asked.

"That's a good question," Daniel admitted, surprised that a talking bird had stumped him. "That's just the way things have always been done."

"Just because things have always been done a certain way doesn't mean that's the best way to do it," the conductor said.

He took his pocket watch out and looked at it. Daniel noticed the inscription on the back of the pocket watch: "Gratitude Time." The conductor and the parrot left without saying another word.

No sooner had Daniel finished reading the back of the ticket than the train let out a whistle and accelerated quickly. It rolled down the tracks—faster and faster and faster. *My*, Daniel thought, *I didn't know steam engines moved so fast . . .*

The train kept going faster until the landscape outside meshed into one giant blur of motion. Then the blur of motion intensified, and the window was almost like a projection on a movie theater screen. Suddenly, the walls of the train dissolved, and Daniel found himself transported back to the recess yard of a grammar school.

Daniel could tell by the angle of the sun that it was early morning. He felt the cool morning air on his face, the ground was slightly dewy, and colorful leaves crunched underfoot. Children's laughter and energy filled the air as they ran around, their breath forming little puffs of mist. *Not any middle school*, Daniel thought, *my school—Latham Middle School.*

Daniel watched his younger self play handball with his friends—the hurried footsteps, the thwap of the ball against palms, and the excited shouts as the children darted back and forth.

Out of the corner of his eye, Daniel saw Andres.

*My gosh*, Daniel thought, *I haven't thought about Andres in years.*

Andres had transferred to the school in

the third grade, after the other children had already formed friend groups. Not only that, but Andres also had a strange accent and jet-black hair with a white streak that started at the hairline above his left eyebrow and arched into the center of his head. Because of these oddities, the children relentlessly teased him.

Andres collected pens—any pens: rusted metal pens, cheap plastic pens he found in empty desks, and fancy pens he'd purchased with his allowance. Daniel watched as Andres walked behind the handball court. Andres tripped and fell, and one of his pens flew out of his pocket and rolled directly to Eric—the biggest bully in school—as if pulled by a magnet. Eric picked up the pen and twirled it between his fingers.

"Give it to me," Andres said. "My pen. It is mine."

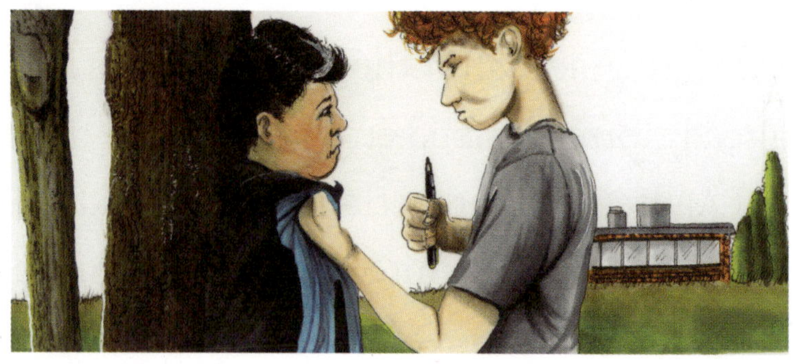

Eric looked at Andres, laughed, and turned away.

Daniel knew what happened next. He remembered it vividly, even all these years later.

Daniel watched as his younger self stopped playing handball and walked over behind Andres.

“Give it back to him,” Daniel said, trying to muster his most confident voice.

Eric scanned his eyes back and forth between Daniel and Andres and chuckled.

“No,” Eric said as he twirled the pen in his outstretched fingers.

“Yes,” Daniel said as he stepped forward.

Eric was speechless, seemingly surprised

that Daniel had challenged him.

He looked back and forth between the two boys again.

For the first time, Daniel could remember, it seemed as if Eric didn't know what to do.

"Fine," Eric said as he dropped the pen on the schoolyard floor. "It's just a stupid pen anyways."

Andres grabbed the pen and hurried into the school.

A few months later, Andres's family moved away, and Daniel never saw him again.

Daniel felt the train hitch, and suddenly, just as if the movie projection had turned off, the scene disappeared, and Daniel found himself back in the train car. The view outside the train window returned to normal, and Daniel felt the train slow down.

The door opened, and the conductor walked in.

"Next stop, Latham."

*Latham?* Daniel thought. *That doesn't make any sense. Latham isn't on the way to Cedarville.*

When the conductor passed, Daniel asked him what kind of train this was.

"I already told you," the conductor said, "the Gratitude Express."

"Okay." Daniel struggled to find the right words. "But what's happening? After you left it felt like I was in a movie, and I was transported back to—"

"How should I know?" the conductor interrupted. "I'm a simple conductor—nothing more, nothing less."

"And I'm just a bird!" the parrot squawked.

"Yes, you're just a bird," the conductor said to the parrot as they walked off.

The train stopped in Latham.

The door to Daniel's car opened, and a man about his age entered and sat across the table from him. The man was immediately familiar and foreign at once; Daniel felt like he was seeing him in both the past and present simultaneously. He knew by the face and the eyes who it was, but in case there was any doubt, the accent and jet-black hair with the white streak gave it away.

"That morning, you altered the course of my life," Andres said. "It wasn't about the pen. It was about the realization that when you confront bullies, they often back down. That moment permanently influenced how I navigate challenges and tough situations."

Andres took a pen out of his pocket and placed it on the table in front of Daniel.

Daniel picked it up.

There was an inscription: *The strong stand up for themselves; the stronger stand up for others.*

"I've always wanted to express my gratitude to you, and now I have."

Without saying another word, Andres stood up and walked out of the train car before a stunned Daniel even had a chance to respond.

# IV

The steam locomotive whistle blared, and the train started moving again. Just as before, it accelerated quickly and kept going faster and faster until the landscape blended into one giant blur of motion and the walls dissolved.

Daniel found himself at a familiar street crossing, although he couldn't quite remember where it was. He watched as an older woman with a bag of groceries slowly made her way across the street. She walked heavily, as if the weight of the world hung on her shoulders; the lines and hollows of her face revealed hardship. As she neared the opposite side of the street, her bag broke, and her groceries scattered everywhere. Two oranges rolled down the curb of the sloped road.

Instead of collecting her scattered groceries, the woman slumped her shoulders, walked to a nearby bench, and wept. All the other pedestrians ignored her plight, but Daniel gathered her groceries in his arms and placed them gently at her feet. When he did so, the woman looked at Daniel with shattered, tearstained eyes.

"I will never forget what you did for me today."

Since her bag was broken and she couldn't carry all her groceries, Daniel helped her carry them three blocks to her apartment. After dropping off the groceries, the woman hugged Daniel wordlessly before he left.

As soon as Daniel watched his younger self leave the woman's apartment, he again felt a hitch and found himself in the train car. The view outside the train window went back to normal.

The door opened, and the conductor walked through.

"Next stop, Silver Springs."

"Silver Springs," the parrot squawked.

*Ahh, yes*, Daniel thought. *That's where I saw the woman drop her groceries, a few blocks from my high school in Silver Springs.*

The train stopped, and an old woman got onto the car and sat down across from him. Daniel didn't remember the woman's face, but he'd never forget her eyes. He was heartened to see that her eyes weren't heavy with tears; they were polished, bright, and gleaming.

"You don't know me—you never even

knew my name—but my name is Beth, and your simple act of kindness saved me that day. It was one of the worst days of my life, and as silly as it sounds, when my bag broke, I felt completely overwhelmed. Your gesture reminded me that there was still goodness and love in the world."

Daniel hadn't thought about that day since it happened, and once again he had no idea the impact his kindness had on another person.

"I wrote this card to you on the day you helped me, but I never knew where to send it. I foolishly hoped I would run into you again at some point, but I never did. It's been sitting on my mantle for years."

She placed the card on the table in the center of the train.

"I'm sorry the card isn't addressed to you. I never even asked your name."

"My name is Daniel." He smiled.

“Thank you, Daniel,” she said and then walked out of the train car.

Daniel opened the card.

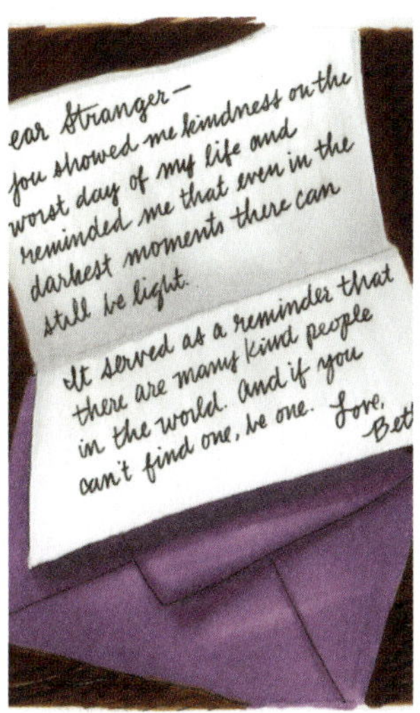


*Dear Stranger,*

*You showed me kindness on the worst day of my life and reminded me that even in the darkest moments there can still be light.*

*It served as a reminder that there are many kind people in the world. And if you can’t find one, be one.*

*Love,*
*Beth*

The train started rolling again, and the conductor and parrot walked in.

"How long until we get to Cedarville?" Daniel asked the conductor. He was enjoying the magical train ride, but he also wanted to see his grandfather.

"Stop after next," the conductor said. "Making all stops!"

Once more, the scenery outside transformed into an indistinct rush of movement, and everything around Daniel faded away. As the walls dissolved, Daniel was transported back to a place he immediately recognized: the office of his first boss after college, Stan.

Daniel saw himself in the office, sitting

across from Stan. Although Stan was his first boss, Daniel always saw him as more of a father figure.

Even though Daniel had become a banker after college, he'd always wanted to be a writer. To inspire himself to write more often, Daniel bought himself an expensive leather binder with his first paycheck. He figured if he had a nice binder to write in, he'd be more inclined to write—and he was right. He wrote before work, after work, and any other time of the day he could.

One day Stan noticed the binder.

"Looks like something a journalist would have."

"Well, I always wanted to be a writer," Daniel blurted out, surprising even himself.

Stan thought for a moment. "Come into my office, Daniel."

Daniel was terrified he'd said too much.

He followed Stan into his office.

"Please shut the door, Daniel," Stan said as he sat across from Daniel and pressed his hands onto his desk. "Now you have to understand that I don't *want* you to leave. You're smart and hardworking and good at your job, and everyone here likes you."

"Thank you."

"But I *do* want you to think about the future. One day, when you look back on your life and career, what do you want to have achieved? Consider the impact you want to have and what you truly want to do."

Daniel didn't say anything.

"You need to figure out what you're good at and what you like to do. Because when you do that, your potential is *limitless*." He paused. "Albert Einstein said, 'Everybody is a genius. But if you judge a fish by its ability to climb a tree, it will live its whole life believing that it is stupid.' And I would add to Einstein's quote, 'Place that fish in water and watch how fast it swims.'"

Daniel nodded.

"A career is too long to do something you are not passionate about, Daniel," Stan said. "You need to find your water."

It was at that very moment that Daniel *finally* felt compelled to leave his banking career and become a professional writer. He owed that transition to Stan. Daniel always regretted not thanking Stan for helping set him on a different course, for shaping his career and life.

When Daniel felt the familiar hitch, he knew what to expect.

The conductor walked through the train and said, "Newburgh City."

"Newburgh City!" the parrot screeched.

When the train stopped, Stan got on. He was older, with a stooped back, but his kind energy and warmth were the same. This time Daniel instinctively knew it was his turn to express gratitude to someone who had influenced his life.

Stan sat down across the table from Daniel.

"Without you I would have never pursued my dream of being a writer. You believed in me, and that inspired me to switch my career," Daniel said.

"I've read all your articles and books. You've become one of my favorite writers," Stan replied. "And each and every time I read your writing, I am so proud of you."

Stan glanced at the leather binder on the table.

"Now it looks appropriate." He smiled.

Instantly, Daniel knew what he wanted to do. He stood up, grabbed the binder, removed his notebook, and handed the binder to Stan. "I want you to have this leather binder as an expression of gratitude. Nobody makes it through this life alone. We're all shaped by the people who've helped us and influenced us."

Stan opened the binder and saw the phrase that Daniel had branded into the inside flap: *Find your water.*

"Thank you. I will always treasure this gift," Stan said. "And I'm glad you found your water." Stan smiled, stood up, and walked off the train.

Although their interaction was brief, expressing his gratitude to Stan brought Daniel a sense of joy, fulfillment, and peace. He'd never realized he'd been carrying around the burden of unspoken gratitude all these years. Hearing others appreciate him and being able to express his thankfulness made him realize how important it was to express gratitude now—what was the point in waiting?

# VI

"Next stop, Cedarville!" the conductor yelled as he entered Daniel's train car.

The conductor, who had been huffing back and forth the entire train ride, finally sat down at the table across from Daniel. He was an older man with a hard, flat face but twinkling eyes.

"What is this train?"

"It's the Gratitude Express."

"Yes, but—"

"The Gratitude Express picks up people who want to express gratitude."

When he said it, the conductor put his hat on the table and flipped it over. Daniel could see what the flipped-over words said: Express Gratitude.

"On the Gratitude Express," the conductor said with a smirk, "people are given a chance to . . . express . . . gratitude."

"Get it?" the parrot squawked. "Get it?"

"Yes, parrot," Daniel said, "I get it."

"Listen, son, as a longtime conductor on the Gratitude Express, I've seen the same assumptions repeatedly: that there'll be more time, that others already know you appreciate them, that you're too young to share your feelings. But the truth is, time is unpredictable, and unsaid words bring pain and regret. It's never too early to express appreciation, but it can be too late. The only real mistake is not speaking up. So for those you love and appreciate, say it now," the conductor said, donned his hat, and left the table.

When Daniel disembarked in Cedarville, the conductor walked off the train with an old leather briefcase.

"Where are you headed next?" Daniel asked.

"The Gratitude Express travels to wherever people want to express . . . gratitude." The conductor smiled. "And our work never ends."

He handed the briefcase to Daniel.

"You nearly forgot this," the conductor said. "It's for you."

Daniel looked at the briefcase with bewilderment. "But it's not mine."

"I didn't say it was yours." The conductor smiled. "I said it was for you."

Daniel looked more closely at the bag and noticed the faded gold initials "WJT" on the side of the briefcase. The initials were familiar to him, but he couldn't explain why. Even if Daniel wanted to look inside the bag, he couldn't, as it was locked, and all the digits were set to 0-0-0-0.

"Well, where did it come from?"

"Sometimes the best things in life are a mystery," the conductor said with a mischievous twinkle in his eye.

Daniel wanted to ask what he should do with the briefcase, but the conductor had already boarded the train, which was chugging out of the station.

Daniel watched as the train huffed around the corner. The billow of smoke was still visible on the horizon.

He turned around and saw a scattering of people at the train station, the first people he'd seen since Beacon.

"Have you ever seen such a thing?" Daniel asked the woman next to him.

"Excuse me?" she said.

"The steam engine, have you ever seen such a thing?"

She looked at Daniel with confused eyes.

"Didn't you just see it pull in?" Daniel asked. "Look."

He pointed to the plume of smoke he had just seen arching into the sky, but there was nothing there.

The woman looked at him and walked away.

Suddenly a comment from the conductor rang in Daniel's head: The Gratitude Express only appears for those who want to express gratitude.

Daniel realized why the Gratitude Express had picked him up. Why hadn't he realized it sooner? Why did he need a talking parrot to point out how foolish a eulogy was? Why was he struggling to write a eulogy when he could tell his grandfather how he felt right now, when it mattered? It was all so obvious.

Daniel opened the notebook—bare now that he'd given the binder to Stan—and looked at the first line again: *Grandpa, you have no idea the difference you've made in my life . . .*

He knew what he had to do: he would tell his grandfather how much he meant to him, and he would do it now.

"It's never too early to tell someone you appreciate them," Daniel said underneath his breath. "But it can be too late."

He closed the notebook, shoved it into the crook of his arm, and walked in the direction of his grandfather's house.

Daniel found his grandfather in his study, sitting in a chair and looking out the window. When Daniel entered, his grandfather turned around. He looked skinny and tired, but the mischievous smile and light in his eyes were still there.

"You have my old briefcase!" his grandfather said, looking at the bag in Daniel's hand. "Where did you find it?"

Suddenly Daniel realized why the faded gold initials on the briefcase were familiar—they were his grandfather's initials. He didn't know how to explain everything that had happened that afternoon and simply shrugged.

"Ahh, no matter." His grandfather grinned. "Sometimes the best things in life are a mystery."

"Indeed." Daniel smiled.

"You know, I could have sworn I heard a steam engine this morning," Daniel's grandfather said as he sat up in his chair. "One of those old-fashioned trains. Maybe I'm imagining things. Yet I assure you, I heard the whistle of a steam train."

Daniel pulled a chair next to his grandfather and looked out the window. The trackless, cornflower blue sky stretched wide across the horizon; the afternoon sun burned hotly in the sky.

"The sound of that steam train brought back memories of my youth and the stories of my life," Daniel's grandfather said as he continued to gaze out the window. There was a buoyancy and energy in his voice that Daniel hadn't heard in a while. "It made me realize that I want to share these stories with you."

While Daniel was eager to hear those tales, he was overwhelmed by a desire to express appreciation for everything his grandfather had done for him.

"Grandpa, there's something I want to say to you, and I want to say it now."

His grandfather turned away from the window and looked at Daniel.

With tears in his eyes, Daniel told his grandfather all the reasons he was grateful for their relationship. Although Daniel had struggled to summarize his feelings toward his grandfather in his notebook, once he started expressing his gratitude, the words flowed freely.

Tears streamed down his grandfather's face as Daniel spoke.

# IX

After Daniel spoke, his grandfather pulled the leather bag into his lap.

"Do you know the code to unlock the briefcase?"

Daniel shook his head.

"Your birthday." His grandfather smiled as he turned the dials to 1-2-1-7.

When his grandfather opened the bag, the smell of old leather and paper filled the air, and dust motes danced up and down in the sunbeams gleaming into the room. Curious, Daniel peeked inside. The briefcase was chock-full of letters; some were in envelopes, some were not. Some were on faded yellow paper that crackled under the fingers of Daniel's grandfather. Others were type-written on fresh white paper.

His grandfather's fingers trembled, and his voice cracked as he read the letters aloud to Daniel.

*Dear William,*

*I've thought about you often since I taught you in the 7th grade. The note you wrote to me at the end of the school year expressing what I had meant to you inspired me to continue teaching for many years and to be the best I could be . . .*

*Dear William,*

*I'll never forget when we were both boys at summer camp and you took me under your wing . . .*

---

*Mr. Thomas,*

*Your support during my college years allowed me to pursue my dream of becoming a nurse . . .*

---

By the time Daniel's grandfather was done reading the letters, the sun had fallen below the tree line, and the room trembled softly in the twilight darkness.

"All I wanted to know was that my life mattered, that I made a difference in the lives of others," his grandfather said as he wiped away more tears.

After Daniel had expressed his gratitude, his grandfather turned his chair to face him, looking directly at Daniel with a newfound sense of vigor. There was a jeweled happiness in his eyes that Daniel hadn't seen in a long time.

"Now it's my turn." He smiled as he grasped Daniel's hand within his own. "Grandson, you have no idea the difference you've made in my life, and I realize now I've never told you why. And if I don't say it now, I know I'll regret having never said it at all. Many unsaid things are lost in the heart . . ."

Tears welled up in Daniel's eyes as he

listened to his grandfather. He experienced the giving and receiving of gratitude, magnifying the impact.

By the time Daniel's grandfather had finished expressing his gratitude, the buzzing twilight had been replaced by the stillness of the stars.

The two men sat there in silence, reveling in the comfort of the profound connection that exists when people express gratitude to one another. Daniel took his grandfather's hand—the skin soft and as thin as paper—and squeezed it in between his own.

As they sat there, hands clasped and hearts united, they heard the distant sound of the Gratitude Express whistle piercing the stillness of the night and saw a majestic plume of steam arching high into the dark sky.

"Where to next?" asked the parrot.

The conductor smiled.

"When one gratitude journey ends, another begins."

# *Epilogue*

*Dear readers:*

*It's incredible to me that people can be so important to us in our lives, and yet we wait until they die to honor and express our profound gratitude to them. This has perplexed me for years.*

*The story of Daniel and his grandfather is actually an evolutionary idea in the making, one that has been in the works for decades. It's become my passion, my bigger why, and it's called Say It Now. This is a movement that has been created for all of us to touch and enlighten all of those who have been important in our lives and, in doing so, fill our lives with gratitude.*

*We all know how unpredictable life can be with millions of lives every year ending abruptly and unexpectedly. Imagine if these people had received a* SAY IT NOW *tribute and learned the impact they had on others. Imagine if the families and friends of these people had been able to express what was in their hearts and minds before it was too late. How would all of their lives have changed?*

*We can't go back in time, but we can embrace these moments moving forward and create a better future. That's what this movement has the power to do.*

*Say It Now is in all fifty US states, in 80,000+ classrooms, and over eighty-three countries on six continents. And it's growing by the minute.*

*Say It Now is for everyone: teachers, coaches, parents, grandparents, mentors, friends, and you.*

*Now it's your moment.*

*So, Say It Now. It's often too late, but never too soon.*

*With deepest gratitude,*

***Walter Green***

**FOUNDER OF THE SAY IT NOW MOVEMENT**

---

For more information on how you can bring **Say It Now** into your life, please visit **justsayitnow.org.**

# Acknowledgments

Before I express my profound gratitude to those who contributed to the writing, illustration, and production of this book, I would be remiss if I didn't credit those who have been an essential part of the evolution of my Say It Now message and movement.

I am very grateful to so many members of my family, my good friends, my mentees, my Young President Organization's forum members, and all those who have touched my life in deep and important ways. Without you there is no book.

One such relationship is Craig Kielburger, co-founder of Legacy+. I first met Craig when he was a teenager some twenty-five years ago. During this time, I have been introduced to and involved with his global initiatives. When I made a commitment to create Say It Now as a global movement, Craig and his organization were my obvious choice to collaborate with on this initiative. The incredible Kerri Stewart, ably supported by James McCowell and a dedicated and talented team at Legacy+, has been instrumental in creating the global impact of this movement.

I have been blessed to have Tucker Stine, my chief operating officer, who has been my invaluable colleague supporting the creation and implementation of all aspects of the Say It Now Movement.

My first book, *This Is the Moment!*, shared the birth of the movement and offered guidance to the reader on how they can initiate their own expressions of gratitude to those who have made a profound difference in their lives. For *The Gratitude Express* I chose storytelling, supported by illustrations, to hopefully inspire you, the reader.

I needed meaningful support to make this book a reality. Joseph Quaderer, a wonderful writer and storyteller, made significant contributions to both the concept development and the writing of the book, for which I am deeply grateful. I felt illustrations would magnify the impact of my message, and Wade Forbes' talents and enthusiasm made that hope a reality.

Quite simply, I had an amazing team committed to both creating the Say It Now Movement as well as producing this book. It has been pure joy to have the opportunity to work with such collegial, competent, and committed people, all of whom wanted to get this message out to the world. Never have I worked with such talented people who left their egos at the door and put their heart and soul into making *The Gratitude Express* and the Say It Now Movement. I am forever grateful.

# About the Authors

## WALTER GREEN

Walter Green's father died when he was a teenager, and it left an indelible impression on him that life is short, precious, and unpredictable. This profound loss magnified his profound appreciation to those who had impacted his life. It also led to his journey of expressing gratitude, which was captured in his first book, *This Is the Moment!: How One Man's Yearlong Journey Captured the Power of Extraordinary Gratitude.*

Walter was Chairman of the Board and CEO of Harrison Conference Services for twenty-five years, which became the leading executive conference center management company in the US. He had been active for years in the Young Presidents Organization and remains a member of the Chief Executives Organization.

Since selling his company, he has devoted himself to supporting various nonprofits, primarily in San Diego, California, with a focus on education and health for the underserved communities. Walter has also been very active mentoring young adults.

He has been an active supporter of Craig and Marc Kielburger, founders of Legacy+, formerly the Free the Children Organization. Walter and his wife were also pioneering supporters of Legacy College, which offers full scholarships and college-level education to hundreds of students in rural Kenya.

Walter lives with his wife, Lola, in San Diego, California.

## JOSEPH QUADERER

Joseph Quaderer is the founder and CEO of Quaderer Media Group, a premier publishing firm serving thought leaders, executives, and public figures. A former Wall Street banker, Joseph brings deep business acumen and a passion for storytelling to every project. His team has helped Fortune 100 CEOs, judges, and entrepreneurs craft impactful books that inspire, inform, and elevate their public presence.

# Join the Say It Now Movement

We hope the story of Daniel inspires you to think about a person or people in your life that have had a significant impact on who you are.

We all know the regret that comes from not expressing our gratitude to that person before they are gone. And now . . . imagine how they would feel knowing how they've shaped you. The more specific the expression of gratitude, the more impactful the gift.

Write a letter. Make a phone call. Send a text. Create a gathering to pay tribute to someone. Or even inscribe a copy of this book as a gift to that person. The intention is the same . . . Say It Now.

We are a global movement that has already inspired over 10,000,000 expressions of gratitude. It doesn't matter how; it matters now. It's your time to Say It Now.

**justsayitnow.org**